AN IMPORTANT MESSAGE TO THE READER

Your mission is to find Captain Blackeye's lost treasure by following the clues throughout the book. But beware! You are about to enter a world of pirates, buried treasure, dastardly deeds and double-crosses. You're not the only one looking for the treasure. Don't trust *anybody*.

You'll play two different parts in this adventure. First, that of a navy spy in the 1780s, paid to keep a close eye on pirates terrorizing the seas. Then, when the action moves forward over 200 years, you will be one of a team of marine archeologists trying to track down the missing treasure today.

On every double page there are questions that need answering. These will guide you in the right direction, but you will have to use your own powers of observation and deduction to solve this baffling mystery. All the vital clues are to be found in the following pages.

Good luck shipmates!

There are helpful hints on page 42 and the answers are on pages 43 to 47. The solution to the whole mystery is on page 48.

REWARD

for creating this book of
EXCITEMENT and WONDER
should go to the following
LADIES & GENTLEMEN:

The Writer, Rupert Heath
The Designer, Becky Halverson
The Photographer, Sue Atkinson
The Editor, Phil Roxbee Cox

With thanks and
PLENTEOUS PRAISE
to all the models and model makers who made this
dramatic work POSSIBLE

Not forgetting
The STUPENDOUS Series Editor
Gaby Waters, of LONDON, England

A VISIT TO THE TAVERN

Time: Saturday, 7:17pm, 23rd July 1785
Place: The Sunny Schooner Tavern, Espinola City

As an undercover agent for the Espinolan Navy, you are reading the orders for your latest top secret mission. They were given to you by the landlord of this dockside tavern. Sipping your tropical fruit punch, you try to figure out the meaning of the song in your orders.

According to the song, where will Blackeye never go?

King Oswald of Espinola needs your help. The pirate Captain Blackeye has stolen a fortune in gold from one of his warships. We think the treasure is still aboard Blackeye's ship, the Disgraceful, currently docked here at Espinola City. International law forbids us from searching a ship while it is docked, but Blackeye will sail tomorrow and bury the gold at a secret location. You must join the crew of the Disgraceful and locate the treasure for us. (Every piece of gold was marked with our national emblem.) We can do the rest.

Little is known about the blackguard Blackeye except that he has a wooden leg and loves whales. He even has a whale tattoo. We have learned that he also has one great fear in life, as told in this song overheard being sung by his men.

Blackeye minds not heading west,
Nor south where swallows fly,
And though he'll gladly sail the east
There's one direction he won't try.

He's heard that there be dragons there
With fiery breath that makes men fry.
The very thought fills him with fear,
That salty seadog, old Blackeye.

Good luck. King Oswald and all Espinola are counting on you.

Admiral Bandybow

Admiral Bandybow
Chief Officer of the Espinolan Navy

3

Crew's Duties, 26th July
Any sailor found shirking will be made to walk the plank.

10am-10.30am Hornpipe dancing

10.30am-11.30am Ginty Widdershin's poetry class in Captain's cabin

11.30am-1.00pm Cut-throat Kevin & Crowsnest Collins: paint cannons red and yellow using special paint

12 midday-1.30pm Scurvy McBurns, Powder Monkey and Samuel 'Shanty' Splicer: swab poop deck.

4.30pm-6pm Powder Monkey's sail-sewing class on foredeck

6pm-8pm Mainbrace splicing for all

9pm Bed

All loose personal items to be removed when working on deck. This avoids damaging the wood and enraging the captain.

4

ALL ABOARD

Time: Tuesday, 12:02pm, 26th July 1785
Place: On the poop deck of the Disgraceful, *under sail*

You've managed to get aboard Blackeye's ship working
as a galley assistant. You've been sent to the poop deck
to fetch some apples from a barrel, stored by the ship's
'duty book'. There's no sign of anyone around, but you
overhear three voices coming from behind a lifeboat.
You catch the words 'chest full of treasure', 'Captain's
cabin' and 'steal for ourselves'.

Who is this whispering trio most likely to be?

PLOTTING AHEAD

Time: Tuesday, 12:18pm, 26th July 1785
Place: The desk in Captain Blackeye's cabin

A tornado is blowing and the cry goes out: 'Batten down the hatches, me hearties!'. You've taken the chance to slip into the captain's cabin to see what you can find. You're facing in the direction the ship is sailing. Before you is a desk with a sea chart and a compass on it.

What is strange about the direction shown on the compass?

OREGANO ISLAND

TARRAGON ISLAND

CINNAMON ISLAND

RUSTICA

ESPINOLA CITY

ESPINOLA

ANTILLIAN

OCEAN

INCENSE ISLAND

CARDAMON ISLAND

SAFFRON ISLAND

N
W
E
S

RIVAL PIRATES IN THESE WATERS

SHARKS

NAVY SHIPS IN THESE WATERS

SEA SERPENTS

MOUSE PRINTS

OUR ROUTE

10

Scurvy

TREASURE TROVE

Time: Tuesday, 12:20pm, 26th July 1785
Place: A Corner of Captain Blackeye's cabin

You throw open the Captain's sea chest and rummage inside. An opened casket is full of gold doubloons. Surely this isn't King Oswald's stolen treasure? And what about that sealed scroll? Something about the design on the seal rings a bell... Before you have time to read it, you hear the thud of footsteps approaching. It's time to make a swift exit.

Whose seal could be on the scroll?

A MIDNIGHT TRIP

Time: Wednesday, 2:42am, 27th July 1785
Place: The Disgraceful's *lifeboat, by lantern light*

After a narrow escape, you hid under a tarpaulin in a lifeboat, and fell asleep. You woke to find the boat being lowered into the sea! You hear voices: the same three pirates you heard on the poop deck are in the boat with you. You can just see one of them holding the casket of gold doubloons from the Captain's sea chest. So far they haven't spotted you...

Who do you think is holding the casket?

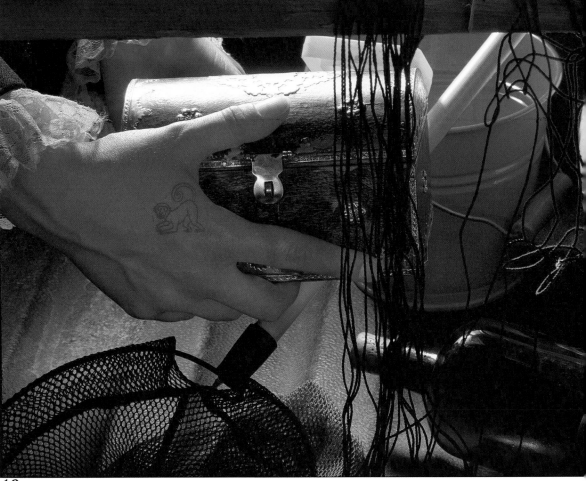

ON THE BEACH

Time: Wednesday, before dawn, 27th July 1785
Place: A desert island, bathed in blue moonlight

When the others leave the boat, you steal after them. In a fruit-filled clearing you see an 'X' marking a spot, and overhear three familiar voices. 'Stop stepping on my feet, Scurvy!' says a woman. 'I can't help where I put my feet, Powder,' replies a gruff voice. 'My shoes are too tight!' pipes up a third. You stare at the one leg you can see.

Who does the leg belong to?

We solemnly take this oath that we will share the treasure equally, and none of us will ever say where it has been buried, even under pain of death, or even worse.
Scurvy
Shanty
Powder
(names signed in ink - Shanty gets faint at the sight of blood)

UNDER ATTACK!

Time: Thursday, 11:12am, 28th July 1785
Place: The deck of the Disgraceful, *in mid-ocean*

Back on board the *Disgraceful*, after another night at
sea, the ship is under attack. While the fighting rages all
around, you are crouched among the wreckage and
dropped weapons. Blackeye's crew is outnumbered and
the ship is sinking...

*Who is the attacking force – a rival gang of pirates or
your naval friends?*

Gold-i-lux
Paint

Ladies' Pistol

Ship's Biscuits

Blackeye's Pistol

THE MERCY OF THE COURT

Time: Thursday, 9am, 11th August 1785
Place: The trial of Blackeye and his crew, High Court,
Espinola City

Two weeks have passed since the Espinolan Navy sank
the *Disgraceful*. At the crew's trial you appear as a chief
witness standing by a table covered in evidence. On it
are all the objects captured from the sinking ship. Scurvy,
Shanty and Powder claim not to remember where they
buried the treasure. Blackeye is keeping tight-lipped.
He says that *all* his personal documents went down
with the ship.

Is he really telling the truth?

Stowaway

Stolen
Papers

Fondant creams are 'root of all evil' says Minister for Law & Order

Fondant creams have been banned from Espinola following a report published by the new Minister for Law & Order, Mr. Joshua 'Iron Fist' Crosspatch.

'I believe that fondant creams are responsible for all the problems in Espinola, so I've made them illegal,' he told reporters at a press conference on Wednesday.

Anyone found in possession of fondant creams is liable ___ rs in prison. Smuggling of f___ ___ms

---

... of the most ruthless buccaneers ever to ___ the seven seas, Captain Barnabas Blackeye ___oday most famous for his daring theft of King ___wald of Espinola's treasure in 1785.

A man of many talents, Captain Blackeye is ___edited as having 'one of ye finest beards of ___s generation', as having invented a very early ___orm of photography and as having 'a most beauteous and thin ankle for such a large man'.

No one knows how Blackeye managed to steal King Oswald's precious gold, and no one knows what became of it.

Some believe that the treasure was later stolen from Blackeye by members of his own rag bag crew.

Following the destruction of Blackeye's ship, the *Disgraceful*, on 28 July 1785, three crew members (Splicer, McBurns and Monkey) claimed to have stolen Blackeye's gold but said that they couldn't remember where they'd buried it.

Another theory is that King Oswald's stolen treasure was melted down, made into one large object and painted over to disguise its true value. The treasure is believed to be worth worth over $5m today.

- 26 -

Captain Blackeye.
Notorious for
stealing King Oswald's treasure.

- 25 -

Pirate's possessions presented to pub

from our own correspondent

A sea chest belonging to the most notorious of all Espinolan pirates, Captain Blackeye, is to be kept in the old sea dog's best-loved watering hole, the *Sunny Schooner Tavern*.

In 1785, the chest was washed up on shore and kept by a local fisherman, Juan Mullett after Blackeye's ship, the *Disgraceful*, was sunk in battle.

A direct descendant of Mr. Mullet presented the chest to the Espinolan government in 1893 and, since then, it has been kept in storage, with the few other items salvaged from the *Disgraceful* including the ship's ___ ___ 'lob book'.

___irate treasure map found in ___

from our life & limb correspondent

A ___olled-up map, believed to show the location of pi___ gol___ worth $5m, has been found in a wooden leg at ___ Espinola Maritime Museum. The leg, which belonged ___ Captain Blackeye, has been in the museum for 150 yea___

'When the leg was taken for cleaning, the map simp___ fell to the floor,' said the curator of limbs, Alfred Elbo___ The map is believed to show a number of island location___ where King Oswald's stolen treasure could be hidden.

'The treasure is part of Espinola's history, and we are determined to claim it back for our country,' said Director___ of Underwater Operations, Dr. John Greygoose. 'We___ start by exploring the area where we believe th___ *Disgraceful* sank. After that, we'll explore the ___ islands marked on the map. These are excitin___

... LifeStyles ...

PEOPLE WITH PIRATES IN THEIR PASTS

by Jane Anchorage

It's strange but true – three descendants of three of the most treacherous members of Captain Blackeye's pirate crew still live and work in Espinola City today.

Lil Monkey, Kurt McBurns and Septimus Splicer may be upright, model citizens, but they are born into families steeped in pirate traditions.

'That must be where I get my love of the sea from,' says Lil Monkey, who works as a diver for the Espinola Maritime Museum. She holds the Pearl Diver Association's coveted Golden Clothespeg Award for holding her breath underwater for six minutes. 'My other passion is eating monkey nuts!' she tells me.

Kurt McBurns owns The Kurt McBurns Wonderful World of Piratical Plunder and Loot, a pirate theme park. 'You can guess where I took the idea from,' he chuckles. The K.M.W.W.P.P. is a tribute to my

ancestor, Scurvy. Not that I like the pirate way of life today!'

The third of the trio, Septimus Splicer, like to keep a low profile – in fact, he wants to disappear. 'I'm a magician,' he explains, 'and I never go anywhere without my pot of vanishing powder. Magic is my life.'

All three are excited at the possibility of Blackeye's treasure being found at last. 'Great publicity for my theme park,' says a happy Mr. McBurns.

Powder

THE FUTURE IS NOW

Time: Monday, 10:36am, 12th May THE PRESENT
Place: Archive Room, Espinola Maritime Museum

Over two hundred years have passed since the sinking of the *Disgraceful*. Your part in the story is now as a marine archeologist – someone who dives for ancient artifacts. You've joined the museum team that is searching for Blackeye's treasure, and start your mission with a little background reading. Hmmm. Blackeye's sea chest sounds interesting.

How did the Espinolan government come by it?

INTERVIEW WITH THE BOSS

Time: Monday, 11:30am, 12th May
Place: Office of the Director of Underwater Operations,
Espinola Maritime Museum

You're standing with Dr. Greygoose behind his desk.
'We sail in three days', he says. 'First, visit the *Sunny
Schooner* tavern to see the chest, then check out the
antiques market ... and don't believe anyone who tells
you pirates don't exist any more. They never died out
around here.' He's one to talk.

What looks suspicious in his office?

FOND?
CREA?

TREASURE TROVE MONTHLY

"FIND OF THE MONTH"

Dr. John Greygoose and Lil Monkey proudly display their latest archeological find. Lil will be accompanying Dr. Greygoose on the mission to recover King Oswald's treasure.

THE TAVERN TODAY

Time: Monday, 3:10pm, 12th May
Place: A table at the all-new Sunny Schooner *Tavern*

Following Dr. Greygoose's instructions, you visit the old tavern. It's the original building, but has become a tourist attraction. You sit at a table covered in local advertisements and dirty plates. You see something which makes you suspect that some familiar names ate at this table before you.

Who could they have been?

Come and See the Figurehead

One of Espinola City's most famous attractions, this is the genuine figurehead from the Disgraceful, Captain Blackeye's ship. The model for the figurehead was the captain's little daughter , Esme. The figurehead was left in the Captain's will to the people of Espinola City. It has now been on display at Espinola City Port for over 200 years.

Scurvy Chili Dog

For one month only, the Sunny Schooner Tavern will give away a Scurvy Chili Dog with every meal purchased. Get your orders in now, shipmates!

Menu

Scurvy Chili Dog
Magic Burger
Pirate's Platter
Submarine Sandwich
Fries
Assorted Nuts

Beverages:
Storm-in-a-Teacup
Schooner of Strawberry Pop
Traditional Lime Juice

A hearty welcome is guaranteed at:

The Kurt McBurns
Wonderful World of
Piratical Plunder and Loot
The most authentic and amazing
Pirate theme park in the world

See you there!

Gold-i-lux Paint

Manufactured in Espinola for over 250 years, this paint is formulated specially to cover 24 carat gold. Guaranteed all-weather protection, no chipping or flaking.

Tried the rest? Buy the best!

FOOD ORDER

2 SC Dogs	3.40
1 M Burger	3.60
1 M Nuts	1.95
Beverages – NIL	
TOTAL	8.95

ny Schooner

Rfad this riddlf if yf bf
Bold fnough to stfal from mf.
Rfmfmbfr now what you arf told:
All that glittfrs is not gold.

If yf wish your coursf sft fair
Look for thf maidfn with goldfn hair.
fool's gold yf will find,
truf trfasurf yf
ffauf bfhind.

THE OLD SEA CHEST

Time: Monday, 3:30pm, 12th May
Place: The attic of the Sunny Schooner *Tavern*

The landlord has been expecting you. He leads you up
to the attic, where Captain Blackeye's old sea chest is
now stored. It is full of items salvaged from the wreck
of the *Disgraceful*. The objects are still bright and
gleaming after over 200 years. Leaving Blackeye's
logbook for later, you eagerly unroll the torn scroll. On
it is a coded message.

Can you decipher what it says?

Or flsf it's foo.
And Oswald's

Esme

IN THE MARKET FOR CLUES

Time: Tuesday, 8:30am,13th May
Place: Mr. Anka's stall, Espinola City Antiques Market

On Dr. Greygoose's advice, you start the day with a visit
to an antiques dealer. He is trying to interest you in an
old model ship. At least it looks more valuable than
that furry parrot. Still, you have seen two things
which could prove important.

What are they?

Examples of pirate gold, melted down and remade into other objects

A MYSTERIOUS MEETING

Time: Thursday, 7am, 15th May
Place: At the port, Espinola City

Today is the day you set off in search of King Oswald's stolen treasure. You decide to stroll around the dock before boarding Dr. Greygoose's ship, the *Aspidistra*. You see him deep in conversation with a man, half-hidden by a basket of fruit. One glimpse of you and they both hurry away.

Any clues to the stranger's identity?
Anything suspicious left behind?

FULL STEAM AHEAD

Time: Thursday, 9:51am, 15th May
Place: In a cabin, aboard the Aspidistra

The search has begun for the sunken wreck of the *Disgraceful*. It's going to be a rough voyage. Even the ship's parrot has turned a little green. You're in a cabin full of crew members' belongings, looking at Blackeye's logbook. After what you've seen, you're suspicious of spies, and something suggests the descendant of Samuel 'Shanty' Splicer is on board!

What is it?

Sunday 23 July - We set sail soon.
I have left behind Disgraceful's figurehead for repainting at Espinola Port. The crew has continued to test the Gold-i-lux paint on board the Disgraceful, and it seems excellent. Soon after leaving sight of land, I discovered I had somehow lost the small cameo brooch I had bought my daughter. To my further disgust, Scurvy was seasick within the first hour of our voyage. I think it's going to be one of those journeys.

Monday 24 July - I have been experimenting with a new kind of picture-making, using a box with a tiny hole in it. I'm thinking of calling my new discovery 'Photo-Graphie'. It might catch on.

Tuesday 25 July - We will soon be in sight of land. We are approaching a group of three islands, called Incense, Saffron and Cardamon. I see from my charts that both Incense and Cardamon are completely surrounded by dangerous looking rocks, so only Saffron Island will be reachable by boat.

26 July - The Disgraceful is under attack!

VANISHING POWDER

GOING DEEP

Time: Thursday, 2pm, 22nd May
Place: A speedboat, off the side of the Aspidistra

You are anchored at the spot where the *Disgraceful*
was believed to have sunk. Everyone is in scuba diving
gear, ready to dive, when by chance you recheck
the oxygen tanks, and discover they are empty.
Someone has tampered with the tanks. Surely none
of your fellow divers can be suspects, as they too
would have drowned.

Or would they?

CATCH OF THE DAY

Time: Thursday, 4:09pm, 22nd May
Place: On the deck of the Aspidistra

The oxygen tanks have been refilled, the first dive has been made, and the haul is spread out on the deck. Nothing here that looks particularly valuable. If only you could be sure that these objects are from the wreck of the *Disgraceful*.

Any clues?

PIRATES

SQUALLS

SAILORS

ADRIFT

LAND AHOY

ON BOARD

BEWARE

AT ANCHOR

SHARKS

AGROUND

• – – / • • • • / • – / – /
– – • / – – – / • / • • • /
– – • • / – – • / • • – /
– • • • / – – • / – – • /
• • – / – • • •

Greetings from Espinola

A • –
B – • • •
C – • – •
D – • •
E •
F • • – •
G – – •
H • • • •
I • •
J • – – –
K – • –
L • – • •
M – –

N – •
O – – –
P • – – •
Q – – • –
R • – •
S • • •
T –
U • • –

ESPINOLA CALLING

Time: Friday, 11am, 23rd May
Place: Radio Room on board the Aspidistra

You are told by one of the crew that there is a message for you in the Radio Room. When you arrive, there is nothing but interference on the radio. An important message has been left nonetheless.

What does the message say?

A Postcard
from
Rustica

E	•	R	•–•
F	••–•	S	•••
G	––•	T	–
H	••••	U	••–
I	••	V	•••–
J	•–––	W	•––
K	–•–	X	–••–
L	•–••	Y	–•––
M	––		

TRICKED!

Time: Friday, 11:15am, 23rd May
Place: In the hold of the Aspidistra

Passing the cargo hold, you spot an empty tea chest, a great clutter of items that have been reported missing from around the ship, and some monkey nuts – Lil Monkey's number one snack. In among the mess is a strangely worded note.

What does the note say?
Which island is likely to be the one mentioned in the note?

Thought ye'd steal my treasure, ye rascals! Well, you're welcome to your fool's gold: all of it! I'll be more than content with what's left behind.

Blackeye

A DEAD END?

Time: Friday, 3:03pm, 23rd May
Place: On Saffron Island

You're too late to stop the modern-day pirates from digging up the casket full of gold. They've gone. The casket has been left behind, along with a few doubloons dropped in a hurry, and this ancient message that was in the bottom. Written in Blackeye's own hand over two hundred years before, it seems to mock all who read it.

If the doubloons aren't King Oswald's stolen treasure, where is it?

HELPFUL HINTS

Pages 2 & 3
Compasses have four points. Which one of these isn't mentioned in the song?

Pages 4 & 5
The answer could lie in the duty book. Think of time and place.

Pages 6 & 7
Look at the sea chart, study the route and don't forget that the arrow on a compass always points north.

Pages 8 & 9
There's a whale symbol on the seal. What have you already read about whales?

Pages 10 & 11
Hands sometimes hold a clue to a person's identity.

Pages 12 & 13
Legs usually come in pairs. Whose could be the exception in this adventure?

Pages 14 & 15
Study the flintlock pistols dropped in the heat of the battle.

Pages 16 & 17
Think back to Blackeye's love of whales.

Pages 18 & 19
The answer lies in one of those articles.

Pages 20 & 21
Look back at the newspaper clippings. One of the items on Dr. Greygoose's desk is very much in the news.

Pages 22 & 23
Any initial thoughts on who ate what?

Pages 24 & 25
Why are there no letter 'e's in this message? The letter 'f' appears rather too much!

Pages 26 & 27
The writing on the scrap of paper looks familiar . . . and the name 'Esme' should be familiar too.

Pages 28 & 29
Two dropped items should help you with the man's identity. As for anything else suspicious, check the fruit.

Pages 30 & 31
Septimus Splicer doesn't like being seen.

Pages 32 & 33
Oxygen lets you breathe underwater. Can you think of anyone who can hold their breath for a long time?

Pages 34 & 35
Could the initial 'C' before Collins stand for Crowsnest? Where have you come across that name before?

Pages 36 & 37
Morse Code isn't the only kind of code used on board the *Aspidistra*.

Pages 38 & 39
Think 'back-to-front'.

Pages 40 & 41
Does the answer lie in an earlier rhyme?

ANSWERS

Pages 2 & 3

The song states that there's one direction Captain Blackeye won't sail because '*He's heard that there be dragons there*'. In the first verse, it's made clear that he doesn't mind sailing west, south or east . . . so that leaves north. This must be the direction that Captain Blackeye will never go.

Pages 4 & 5

The time now is 12:02pm. According to the duty book, the only people with duties on the poop deck at the moment are Scurvy McBurns, Powder Monkey and Samuel Shanty Spicer. Apart from you, there's no one else around and the threat in the book that '*Any sailor found shirking will be made to walk the plank*' suggests that these three sailors are likely to be where they're supposed to be!

It's possible that some of the items left by the duty book belong to the whispering trio.

Pages 6 & 7

On the chart is a red dotted line which, according to the key, is 'OUR ROUTE'. If this is meant to be the course that the *Disgraceful* is now taking, then it is odd for two reasons. First, because the marked course shows us going north – a direction we know the Captain won't travel from the song on page 3. Second, although you are facing the direction in which the ship is sailing, the compass shows north to be in the opposite direction. The *Disgraceful* is, in fact, heading southward.

Pages 8 & 9

The seal on the scroll has the imprint of a whale on it. In your orders from Admiral Bandybow on page 3, you are told that the Captain loves whales and that he even has a whale tattoo – this suggests that the seal is probably Blackeye's.

Pages 10 & 11

From their voices, you know that the three pirates in the lifeboat with you now are the same three you overheard whispering on the poop deck. You suspected then that they were Scurvy McBurns, Powder Monkey and Samuel 'Shanty' Spicer. The hand holding the casket of doubloons has a small monkey tattooed on it and, of the three suspects, Powder Monkey seems the most likely candidate to have such a tattoo.

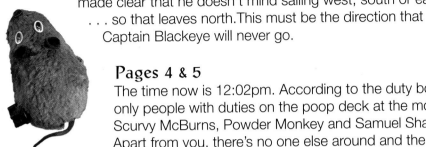

Pages 12 & 13

You know from the conversation between the three pirates from the lifeboat that they each have *two* legs – but the person in front of you has one 'real' leg and a wooden leg. The only person you know who has a wooden leg is Captain Blackeye himself (something you originally learned in your orders on page 3).

The note confirms that you were correct in identifying the three poop deck plotters.

Pages 14 & 15

It is most likely to be the Espinolan Navy. On the butt of one of the flintlock pistols – dropped on the deck in the heat of the battle – is a ship's wheel design. This matches the design on the seal attached to your orders (on page 3) from Admiral Bandybow of the Espinolan Navy.

Pages 16 & 17

Not surprisingly, the pirate Captain is lying. The scroll with the whale seal, sticking out of the books, looks suspiciously like the one you spotted in his sea chest before the ship went down.

Pages 18 & 19

The answer lies in the newspaper article headed **'Pirate's possessions presented to pub'**. According to this, Blackeye's sea chest was washed up on shore after the sinking of the *Disgraceful* in 1785 and found by a fisherman named Mullet. In 1893, Mullet's descendant presented the chest to the Espinolan government.

Pages 20 & 21

You learned from an article on pages 18 & 19 that the Espinolan Minister for Law & Order has banned fondant creams as the **'root of all evil'**. Anyone in possession of fondant creams is liable to go to prison . . . yet Dr. Greygoose appears to have a box of fondant creams – half hidden by his hanky – on his desk!

Pages 22 & 23

It seems that you've been sitting at a table that the descendants of Powder Monkey, Scurvy McBurns and Samuel 'Shanty' Splicer were eating at earlier. From the newspaper clipping headed **PEOPLE WITH PIRATES IN THEIR PASTS**, you know that their names are Lil Monkey, Septimus Splicer and Kurt McBurns.

Their initials – L.M., S.S. and K.M. – match the initials written next to the food orders. (It appears that one of them was working out who-spent-what on the meal.) As if that isn't enough, the initials L.M. appear by the order of monkey nuts – which Lil Monkey describes, in the same clipping, as being her '**other passion**'.

Pages 24 & 25

The poem is in straightforward English, except for the occasional '*ye*' – which is old English for the word 'you' – and the fact that all letter 'e's have been changed to 'f's. There is also a piece missing.

Once the 'e's have been returned to their proper places, what's left of the message reads:

> *Read this riddle if ye be*
> *Bold enough to steal from me.*
> *Remember now what you are told:*
> *All that glitters is not gold.*
> *If ye wish your course set fair*
> *Look for the maiden with golden hair*
> *. . . . gold ye will find*
> *. . . . true treasure ye leave behind*

Pages 26 & 27

The two most important items are the piece of yellowed paper and the locket. The piece of paper is the missing corner of Captain Blackeye's poem on page 24. Once the scrap has been added to the last three lines and decoded, the message ends:

> *Or else it's fool's gold ye will find*
> *And Oswald's true treasure ye leave behind.*

The locket could well have belonged to Captain Blackeye himself. According to an advertisement about the *Disgraceful*'s figurehead on page 22, he is said to have had a daughter called Esme – the name which appears next to the picture of the girl in the locket.

Esme

Pages 28 & 29

The sailing cap dropped on the ground looks remarkably like the one worn by Kurt McBurns on the front of his leaflet about '*The Kurt McBurns Wonderful World of Piratical Plunder and Loot*' pirate theme park, on page 23.

There is also a business card with the initials *K.M.W.W.P.P.L.* printed on it – the initials Kurt uses as a shortened version of his theme park in a newspaper article on page 19.

Sticking out of a basket of fruit is the corner of a box with a very familiar pattern on it. It looks identical to the illegal box of fondant creams that was half-hidden on Dr. Greygoose's desk on page 21.

Pages 30 & 31

In Jane Anchorage's article on page 19, Septimus Splicer is quoted as saying: 'I'm a magician and I never go anywhere without my pot of vanishing powder.'

There is a pot of vanishing powder on the bed!

Pages 32 & 33

In a newspaper article on page 19, it is stated that Lil is 'a diver for the Espinola Maritime Museum' – the organization you're working for under Dr. Greygoose. It also states that she 'holds the Pearl Diver Association's coveted *Golden Clothespeg Award* for holding her breath underwater for six minutes'.

This suggests that Lil Monkey would be in the least trouble if she went diving without oxygen.

Pages 34 & 35

The plunger has 'PROPERTY OF C.COLLINS' written on it (in long-lasting waterproof ink!). In the *Disgraceful's* dutybook, which appears on pages 4 & 5, the name '*Crowsnest Collins*' appears under 11:30am cannon painting – fortunately, the book was saved according to the clipping entitled '**Pirate's possessions presented to pub**' on page 18.

C. COLLINS could very possibly be Crowsnest Collins, so these items *are* likely to be from the wreck of the sunken *Disgraceful*.

Pages 36 & 37

There are, in fact, three coded messages waiting for you in the Radio Room. Two can be deciphered using the Morse Code keys pinned to the wall.

Once decoded, the first of these, **MORSE CODE MESSAGE NO. 1**, is the question 'WHAT GOES ZZUB ZZUB' and the second, **MORSE CODE MESSAGE NO. 2**, is the answer 'A BEE REVERSING'. They must be some kind of a joke!

The third message is in the form of three flags on the desk. Once decoded using the key pinned to the wall in the top left-hand corner, they read: BEWARE PIRATES ON BOARD. But there is nothing to suggest who the warning is from.

Pages 38 & 39
The note is, in fact, in a very simple code. The words are in the same order that they would be in an ordinary message – it's just that the order of the *letters* in each word have been reversed. Decoded, the message reads:

GONE TO DIG UP TREASURE ON ISLAND
LIL, SEPTIMUS AND KURT
P.S. HOPE YOU LIKED OUR MESSAGES IN THE RADIO ROOM

They have probably gone in search of the treasure on Saffron Island because, according to Captain Blackeye's logbook entry on page 31, Incense Island and Cardamon Island are both completely surrounded by dangerous rocks and *'only Saffron Island will be approachable by boat'*. This must be where the original Monkey, McBurns and Splicer buried the casket of doubloons over two hundred years ago.

Pages 40 & 41
To be able to answer the question *'Where is King Oswald's treasure?'* you must first be sure *what* it is. Blackeye's latest note suggests that the doubloons aren't his real treasure . . . but are there any clues earlier in the adventure that might back up this statement? Try looking at pages 34 & 35 again.

Once you think you know where King Oswald of Espinola's stolen treasure is hidden, then – and only then – turn the page and hold the solution up to a mirror . . .

THE SOLUTION

King Oswald's stolen treasure is certainly not in the possession of Lil Monkey, Kurt McBurns or Septimus Splicer. The gold doubloons in the small casket they dug up on Saffron Island were never a part of King Oswald's treasure. Blackeye wasn't lying when he referred to them in his note on page 40 as 'fool's gold'.

In your orders on page 3, Admiral Bandybow of the Espinolan Navy says that every piece of gold from King Oswald's stolen treasure, 'is *marked with our National emblem*'. These doubloons are, however, marked with a special cross – similar to one that appears on a bottle of grog on page 34. The grog is '**Made in Rustica**' and '**Bears Rustican national emblem**'. You can see from the chart, on page 7, that Rustica is a separate country from Espinola. Therefore, since the doubloons carry the Rustican emblem, they can't be King Oswald's treasure.

So where is the real treasure? Captain Blackeye left plenty of clues. Once decoded, the message on page 24 says, '*Look for the maiden with golden hair*.' The only girls with golden hair are Esme, Blackeye's daughter, whose picture appears in the locket on page 26, and the figurehead which used to be on the front of Blackeye's ship, the *Disgraceful*. According to the advertisement on page 22, the Captain's little daughter Esme was the model for the figurehead.

In his entry in the logbook shown on page 31, Blackeye states that he '*left behind Disgraceful's figurehead for repairing at Espinola Port*'. He then writes about testing '*Gold-i-lux*' paint. In the duty book on page 4, two pirates are listed to '*paint cannons red and yellow using special paint*'. A red and yellow tin of '*Gold-i-lux*' paint appear on the deck on page 15. In an advertisement on page 23 '*Gold-i-lux*' is described as being specially formulated '**to cover 24 carat gold**' . . . So, according to the logbook, the figurehead of Blackeye's ship has been removed and is being painted with a special paint designed to cover gold.

On page 18, the article about Captain Blackeye in the book says: '*Another theory is that King Oswald's treasure was melted down, made into one large object and painted over to disguise its true identity*.' This theory was correct.

Captain Blackeye removed the figurehead from his ship, had King Oswald's treasure melted down and shaped like the missing figurehead – then had it painted to look like the original. Because he was captured, the pirate captain could never retrieve the golden figurehead. And where is it now? As the advertisement says on page 22, the figurehead is on show at Espinola City Port . . . King Oswald's treasure has been right under everyone's nose all the time!

First published in 1995 by Usborne Publishing Limited, Usborne House, 83-85 Saffron Hill, London EC1N 8RT, England.
© Copyright 1995 Usborne Publishing Ltd.